Marc Kielb...
Everyone's B...
A Kid's Adventure in Thailand

ILLUSTRATED BY MARISA ANTONELLO & VICTORIA LAIDLEY

That's why we work with lots of children in Canada, the United States and United Kingdom who learn about the reasons why children in other parts of the world can't go to school or why the water they drink is unsafe and unclean.

Then they hold events to teach other people about these issues and raise money to send to countries like India, Kenya, Haiti, and Ecuador.

But when I was younger, the problems of the world seemed like they were

TOO BIG!

But one day, a mentor asked,
WHAT KIND OF PERSON DO YOU WANT TO BE?
My hand stayed down because I didn't know the answer.
HUH?
I ♥ STUDENT COUNCIL!
HOW TO GET INVOLVED
and involved, and involved, and involved...
101 WAYS TO LOVE ALGEBRA!
GEOGRAPHY: A LOVE STORY
REVISED EDITION
BURP!

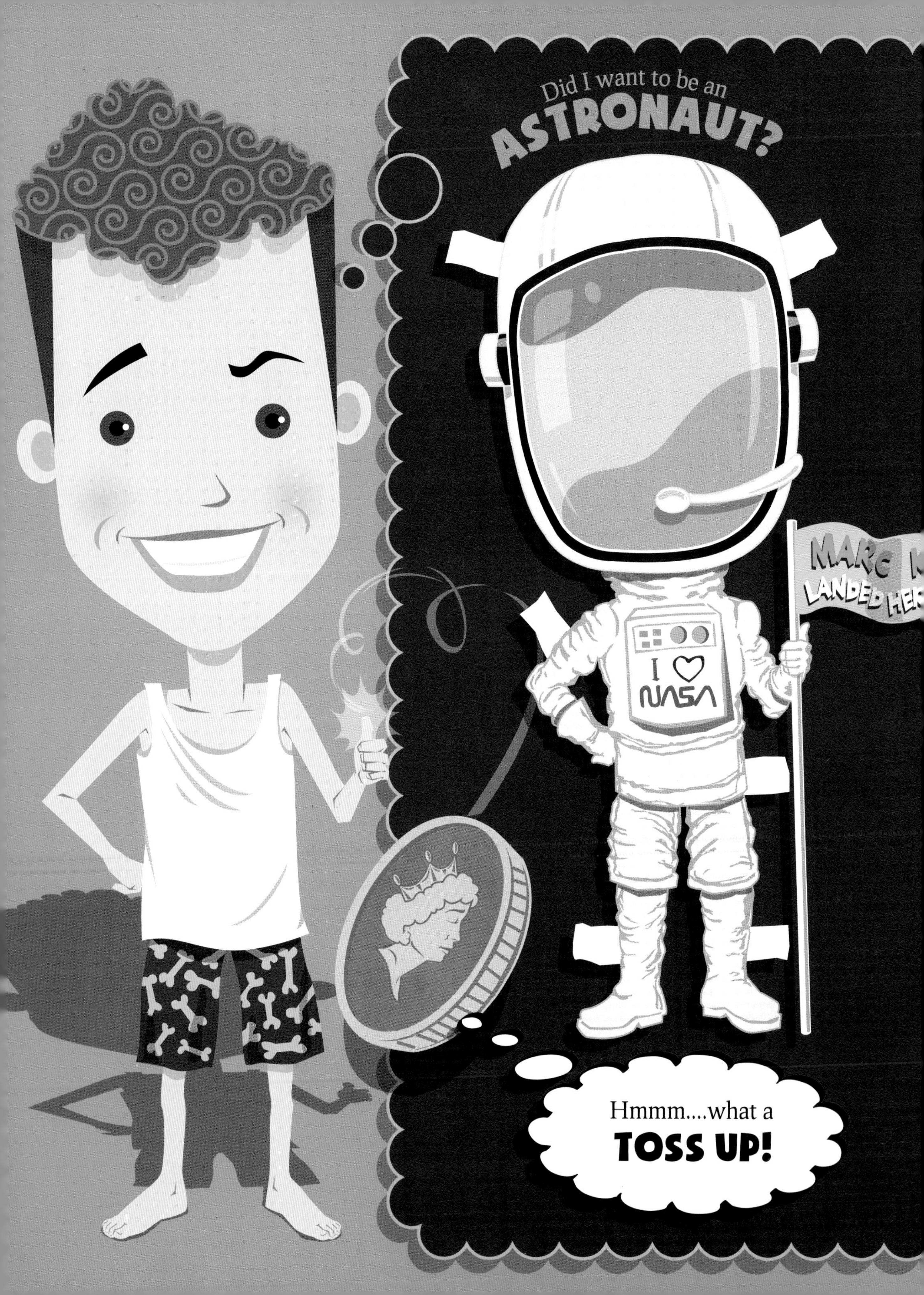
Did I want to be an
ASTRONAUT?
I ♡ NASA
Hmmm....what a
TOSS UP!

WOW!

When I arrived in the capital city of **BANGKOK,** I was both nervous and excited. There was so much to see everywhere I looked. Thousands of motorcycles, mopeds and brightly painted taxis—called **TUK TUKS**—crowded the streets.

Everyone and everything seemed to move so fast, except for the elephants. Two elephants slowly paraded down the street, past the

BUDDHIST MONKS

who walked together, collecting donations.

Small boats sailed on the river in the distance...

...and stall after stall of food lined the sidewalks.

Then my taxi entered Klong Toey...

For as far as I could see, there were small homes made of wood, tin and cardboard. There were piles of garbage everywhere. And the open sewers smelled terrible. Clothes were drying on clotheslines just outside the houses.

People were everywhere. Grandmothers and grandfathers sat quietly, just inside doorways and moms were cooking what little food they had.

All these people lived on less than one or two dollars a day!

At home, I wouldn't even be able to buy a comic book or sandwich for that much money.

My heart sank.

I was seeing poverty for the first time and it made me sad. I didn't know if I was strong enough to stay there.

I ran to my tiny apartment and started to repack my bag. I tried not to cry as I called my parents to tell them I was coming home. I couldn't wait to leave.

Just then, there was a knock at the door...

During the next few days, I met Tep's friends. They taught me very basic Thai. Words like:

I watched the boys and girls run around in bare feet, trying to earn a small living by shining shoes. What inspired me most was how they shared everything with each other, looking after one another like a family does.

A few days later, I set out for the party. When Tep and the other children saw me, they shouted with delight.

We all sang "**HAPPY BIRTHDAY**" together and laughed loud and long when everyone said someone else's name during the singing. After the feast of peanuts and watermelons, there was dancing, storytelling, and much more laughter.

I was used to birthday parties with mountains of presents. But these children were so happy without the presents. They didn't have parents or a home or even enough food to eat, but that didn't stop them from being happy.

Though they'd never know it, it was these young children who convinced me to stay in Klong Toey.

I taught English to schoolchildren and played soccer with the street kids every morning.

They changed my life.

As I left from Thailand almost one year later, I thought about the question that had started my journey:

WHAT KIND OF PERSON DO YOU WANT TO BE?

I was much closer to the answer.

I realized that some problems can be so big, we feel like we can't do anything about them. But learning about people, hearing their stories and caring enough to do something small—like coming together to celebrate each other's birthday— could make the world of difference in someone's life.

ME TO WE BOOKS

LESSONS FROM A STREET KID

Craig Kielburger;
Illustrated by Marisa Antonello and Victoria Laidley

After starting Free The Children when he was twelve years old, Craig Kielburger continued his adventure in Brazil. It was on the streets of Salvador, Brazil, that Craig learned the firsthand stories of street children. In this easy-to-read, full-colour illustrated children's book, the reader learns about the joys of these very children. A cut above your typical children's book, this true story culminates in a soccer game using a plastic bottle as a ball.

MY MAASAI LIFE:
A CHILD'S ADVENTURE IN AFRICA

Robin Wiszowaty;
Illustrated by Marisa Antonello and Victoria Laidley

Follow a young Robin Wiszowaty as she travels to Kenya for the first time. Living with the Maasai people, Robin explores the land with her new family. Getting water, finding wood and singing songs. And don't forget the zebras, cows and giraffes. It is all a part of the adventure with the Maasai. With Robin as a guide, the full-color illustrations only enhance any child's own adventure into the world of the Maasai.

IT TAKES A CHILD

Craig Kielburger and Marisa Antonello;
Illustrated by Turnstyle Imaging

It was an ordinary morning like any other. Twelve-year-old Craig Kielburger woke to his alarm clock and hurried downstairs to wolf down a bowl of cereal over the newspaper's comics before school. But what he discovered on the paper's front page would change his life—and eventually affect over a million young people worldwide. It Takes a Child is a fun, vibrant look back at Craig's adventures throughout South Asia, learning about global poverty and child labor. This incredible story truly demonstrates you're never too young to change the world.

MY MAASAI LIFE: FROM SUBURBIA TO SAVANNAH

Robin Wiszowaty

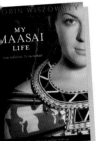

In her early 20s, Robin Wiszowaty left the ordinary world behind to join a traditional Maasai family. In the sweeping vistas and dusty footpaths of rural Kenya, she embraced a way of life unlike she'd ever known. With full-color photographs from her adventures, Robin's heart-wrenching story will inspire you to question your own definitions of home, happiness and family.

THE WORLD NEEDS YOUR KID: RAISING CHILDREN WHO CARE AND CONTRIBUTE

Craig Kielburger and Marc Kielburger and Shelley Page

This unique guide to parenting is centred on a simple but profound philosophy that will encourage children to become global citizens. Drawing on life lessons from such remarkable individuals as Jane Goodall, Mia Farrow and Archbishop Desmond Tutu, award-winning journalist Shelley Page and Marc and Craig Kielburger demonstrate how small actions make huge differences in the life of a child and can ultimately change the world.

FREE THE CHILDREN

Craig Kielburger

This is the story that launched a movement. Free the Children recounts twelve-year-old Craig Kielburger's remarkable odyssey across South Asia, meeting some of the world's most disadvantaged children, exploring slums and sweatshops, fighting to rescue children from the chains of inhumane conditions. Winner of the prestigious Christopher Award, Free the Children has been translated into eight languages and inspired young people around the world.

STANDING TALL: MY JOURNEY

Spencer West

Navigating life on his hands, Spencer has always lived with purpose. But living in a world where society seems to dictate happiness, Spencer wanted more out of life than just a paycheck and material possessions. He wanted to have an impact, but wasn't always sure how. That was until he had the epiphany that being different was for a reason. This is the candid, coming-of-age story of a young man's journey of working hard, laughing a lot and always standing tall.

Visit www.metowe.com/books to learn more.

ME TO WE TRIPS

If you have a son or daughter who wants to really experience another culture and truly see the world, go on a Me to We trip together. Seek out a volunteer travel experience as a family and see breathtaking Kenya. Our staff live and work in the communities that are visited, coordinating schoolbuilding and supporting development in participation with local communities. Me to We trips teach leadership skills, help forge truly meaningful connections and offer profound cultural experiences. Over 3,000 adventurous people of all ages have chosen to volunteer abroad with us. Experience incredible activities like building schools and assisting on clean water projects. Meet exuberant children excited at new possibilities for learning and immerse your family in local communities in ways never thought possible. Activities that truly bind a family. And best of all, cherish memories that will last a lifetime.

To learn more, visit: www.metowe.com/trips

ME TO WE SPEAKERS

Bring me as a speaker to your kid's school – and let them take away all they need to "be the change." The speaking team at Me to We has traveled the world to discover the most inspirational people with remarkable stories and life experiences. From community activists to social entrepreneurs, our roster of energetic, experienced speakers are leading the Me to We movement: living and working in developing communities, helping businesses achieve social responsibility and inspiring auditoriums of youth and educators to action. Our stories and powerful messages inspire, motivate and educate. We leave young and old audiences alike with a desire to take action and make a difference. We make them laugh, cry and gain new perspective on what really matters. Be warned: our passion is contagious.

To learn more, visit: www.metowe.com/speakers